Bathwater's Hot

Shirley Hughes

WALKER BOOKS
LONDON

Bathwater's hot,

Seawater's cold,

Ginger's kittens are *very* young

But Buster's getting old.

Some things you can throw away,

Some are nice to keep.

Here's someone who is wide awake,

Shhh, he's fast asleep!

Some things are hard as stone,
Some are soft as cloud.

Whisper very quietly . . .

SHOUT OUT LOUD!

It's fun to run very fast

Or to be slow.

The red light says 'stop'

And the green light says 'go'.

It's kind to be helpful,

Unkind to tease,

Rather rude to push and grab,
Polite to say 'please'.

Night time is dark,

Day time is light.

The sun says 'good morning'

And the moon says 'good night'.